MY FIRST TRAIN TRIP

A Grosset & Dunlap **ALL ABOARD BOOK**®

For my brother Doug—E.N.

To Nick, Meredith, and all of Amtrak.
We thank you—E.H.

Text copyright © 1999 by Grosset & Dunlap. Photographs copyright © 1999 by Elizabeth Hathon. All rights reserved. Published by Grosset & Dunlap, a member of Penguin Putnam Books for Young Readers, New York. GROSSET & DUNLAP is a trademark of Grosset & Dunlap, Inc. ALL ABOARD BOOKS is a trademark of Grosset & Dunlap. Registered in U.S. Patent and Trademark Office. THE LITTLE ENGINE THAT COULD and engine design are trademarks of Platt & Munk, Publishers, a division of Grosset & Dunlap. Published simultaneously in Canada. Printed in the U.S.A.

Library of Congress Cataloging-in-Publication Data
Neye, Emily.
    My first train trip / by Emily Neye ; photographs by Elizabeth Hathon.
      p. cm. — (A Grosset & Dunlap all aboard book)
    Summary: Photographs and text depict the excitement of a boy's first train trip as he meets the conductor and engineer, eats in the dining car, and goes to bed in the sleeping car.
    [1. Railroads—Trains Fiction.] I. Hathon, Elizabeth, ill. II. title. III. Series.
PZ7.N4878My   1999
[E]—dc21   99-37709
                                             CIP

ISBN 0-448-41998-X   A B C D E F G H I J

My First Train Trip

By Emily Neye

Photographs by
Elizabeth Hathon

Grosset & Dunlap, Publishers

Mom and I are going on a trip to visit my grandma. She lives far away, so we are taking a train. We will be on the train all night!

The train station is a big place. First we go to pick up our tickets. Then we check the departures screen. There are no delays. Our train will be leaving soon!

We walk out to the end of the platform to wait. Mom asks me if I can see the train coming. "Yes! There it is!" I say.

But it's moving so slowly! It seems like it will never get here.

Finally, it pulls into the station. This workman tells me that his crew will make sure the train is ready for our trip. They will check all the cars and the links between them.

But all of a sudden, I'm feeling nervous. I don't know if I want to be on a train all night long! Maybe I should stay right here….

But Mom takes my hand and leads me over to the train. "Don't worry, it's going to be fun. I promise!" She talks to the porter to see how much time we have before the train leaves.

Then she takes me up to talk to the engineer. He is the driver. There are lots of controls in his part of the train.

Hey, I like the view from up here! Maybe this trip will be fun after all.

When we go back out to get on the train, we meet a conductor. He helps us find the car with our seats.

He even lets me try on his hat! Maybe I'll be a conductor someday, too.

The crew has finished checking the train. "Looks good!" this man signals.

All aboard! We walk down the platform to our car.

We go back to our own special room. This is where we will sleep tonight. Mom told me what it would be like, but I'm happy to see it for myself. It's just the right size for the two of us.

Soon we have a visitor. Mom tells him this is my first train trip. I show him my teddy. I brought my bear along because he is dressed like an engineer.

We read for a little while, but I'm curious about the other cars. "Let's find seats by a window before the train leaves," Mom says.

We find seats near the front of the train and another conductor comes around to take our tickets. She tells us the trip will take fifteen hours!

She knows it is my first train trip, too—she gives me a special hat! It looks just like an old-fashioned engineer's cap.

I tell her that Mom probably wants one, too. Now we both are ready to go!

Chug-chug-chug. We start to pull out of the station. I wave to the other trains.

Grandma, here we come!

There are tables in front of our seats that we can pull down. Some people use their trays for computers or books.

We brought lots of things to do in our bags. First, Mom and I play cards with Freddy. We play my favorite game—Go Fish!

Soon it is time for a little supper. There is a snack bar and a restaurant right on board. Mom and I walk back to the snack bar. We choose some chips, sandwiches, and drinks.

Then we walk back to our seats. Mom has to be careful not to spill!

After we eat, I get a little bit restless. I decide to
walk around the train. It feels good to stretch out.

It's fun to look out different windows. Freddy wants to have a look, too.

Now it's time for bed, so we head back to our room. While we were gone, this porter turned our seats into beds!

Mom and I get into our pajamas. We wash up in our own mini-bathroom. I brush my teeth and wash my face. My new teddy needs his face washed, too.

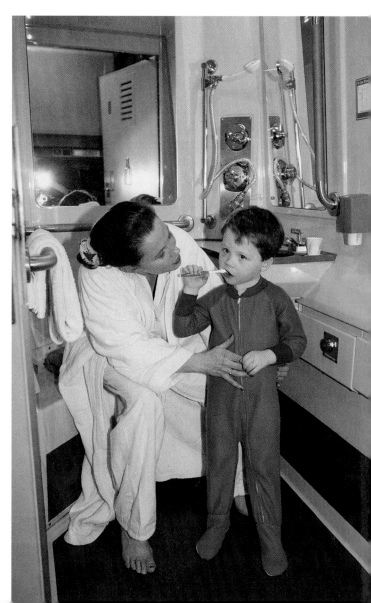

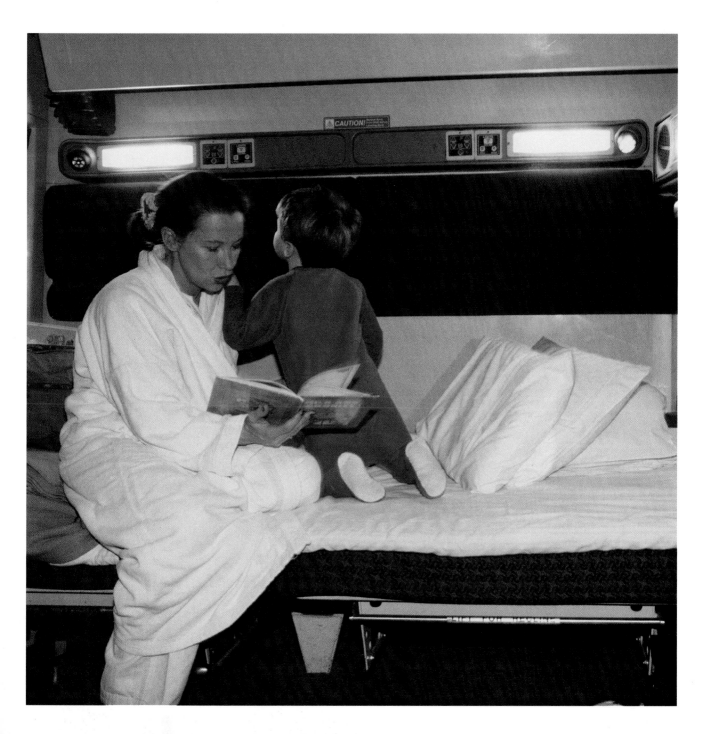

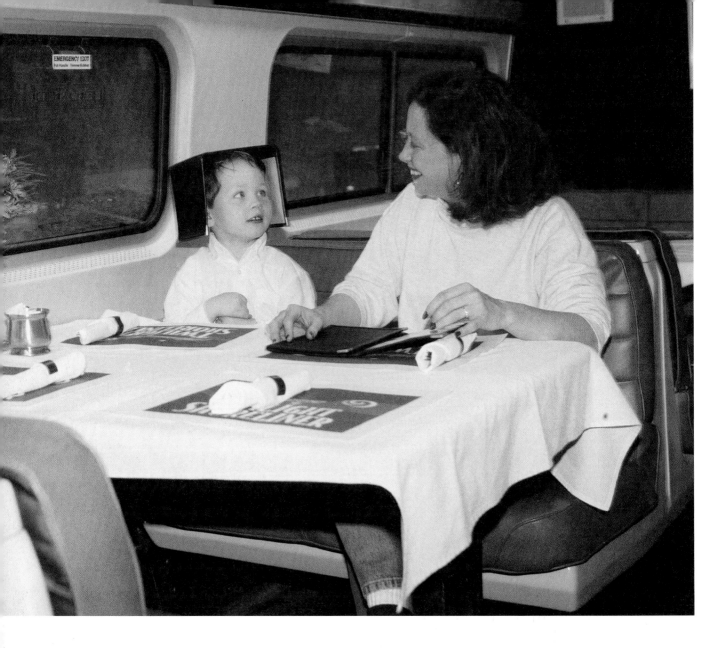

Before I know it, it's morning! We get dressed and go to the dining car for some breakfast. I get silly at the table— I'm so excited to see Grandma.

We have a hot breakfast that was cooked right on board.
Mom tells me we will be there very soon.

Here we are!

And there is Grandma. She has been waiting for us at the station.

"Thank you for coming so far to see me," she says.
"You must be tired after such a long trip!"

But I'm not tired. I can't wait for the train trip home!